Extreme Sports

skate boarding

ALLAN MOREY

BLACK RABBIT BOOKS

Bolt is published by Black Rabbit Books
P.O. Box 227, Mankato, Minnesota, 56002
www.blackrabbitbooks.com

Alissa Thielges, editor; Michael Sellner, designer
and photo researcher

Library of Congress Cataloging-in-Publication Data
Names: Morey, Allan, author.
Title: Skateboarding / Allan Morey.
Description: Mankato, Minnesota: Black Rabbit Books, [2024] | Series: Extreme sports | Includes bibliographical references and index. | Audience: Ages 8–12 | Audience: Grades 4–6 | Summary: "Get your heart pumping with the extreme sport of skateboarding. Struggling and reluctant readers will discover the skills and equipment needed to catch big air. Includes a table of contents, glossary with pronunciations, further resources, and an index"— Provided by publisher.
Identifiers: LCCN 2023008863 (print) | LCCN 2023008864 (ebook) | ISBN 9781623108854 (library binding) | ISBN 9781623108991 (pdf)
Subjects: LCSH: Skateboarding—Juvenile literature.
Classification: LCC GV859.8 .M68 2024 (print) | LCC GV859.8 (ebook) | DDC 796.22—dc23/eng/20230228
LC record available at https://lccn.loc.gov/2023008863
LC ebook record available at https://lccn.loc.gov/2023008864

Printed in China

Image Credits

Alamy: Aflo Co. Ltd. 21, Dynamicfoto 9 (b), dzmat.ph 8, evan Hurd 24 (Brown), G Scammell 15, urbanbuzz 1; Dreamstime: Mark Vorobev 7, Yuliya Pauliukevich 16–17 (ramps); Getty: Christopher Polk 25 (Burnquist), Francois Nel cover, Jeff Gross 4–5, 6, picture alliance 22 (b), RJ Sangosti 26–27, Xinhua News Agency 22 (t); Lance Group (Way); iStock: lzf 9 (t), skodonnell 12–13; Lush Longboards 24–25 (Connelly); Shutterstock: DenisNata 19 (t), focuslight 19 (bm), Garna Zarina 18 (l), 19 (bl), Nebojsa S 16 (dark blue), OSTILL is Franck Camhi 31, PavelStoker 16 (pink), 17 (orange, yellow), shurkin_son 14, 16 (light blue), 17 (purple), Smile19 3, 32; XGAMES 25 (Bufoni), 28

Contents

CHAPTER 1

Dropping In

A skateboarder hops on her board. She leans forward and drops into the **half-pipe**. She speeds down one side and up the other side. After a nose stall, she drops back down.

Back and forth, she crosses the half-pipe. One time she does a **kickturn**. Another time she rocks to **fakie**. She builds up speed to hit an extreme trick.

187
KILLER PADS

Catching Air

The next time she skates up, she catches air. She grabs the board and spins a frontside **360**. Then she drops down and does a fly out on the far side of the half-pipe. CLUNK! She sticks the last trick!

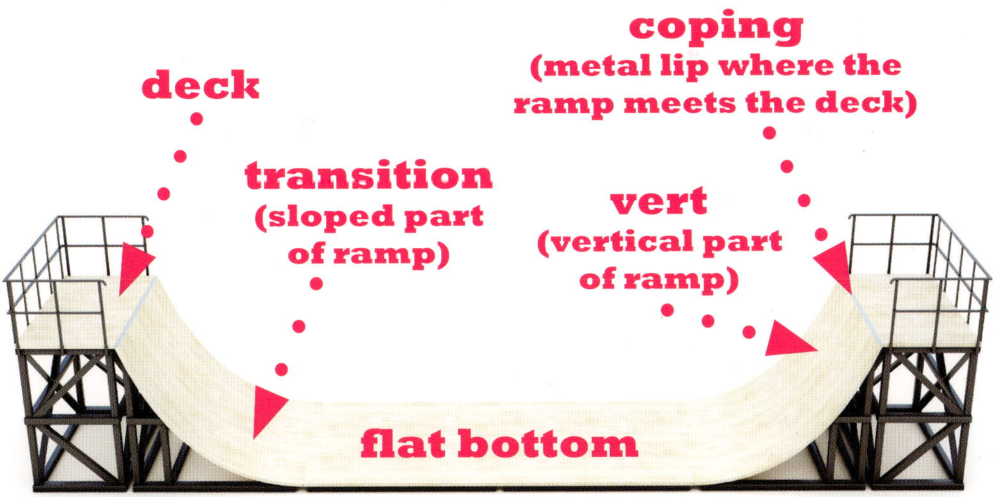

Half-Pipe

CHAPTER 2

The Sport of Skateboarding

Skateboarding is more than just hopping on a board. There are different styles and types of skateboards. Double kick and longboards are the most common. They are used for the most extreme tricks. Longboards are great for **bombing** downhill.

Types of Skateboards

double kick
short deck with curved ends and small, hard wheels; best for tricks

cruiser
wide deck with tail curved up and large, soft wheels; good for "cruising" around

longboard
long, flat deck with large, soft wheels; fastest board

SKATEBOARD PARTS

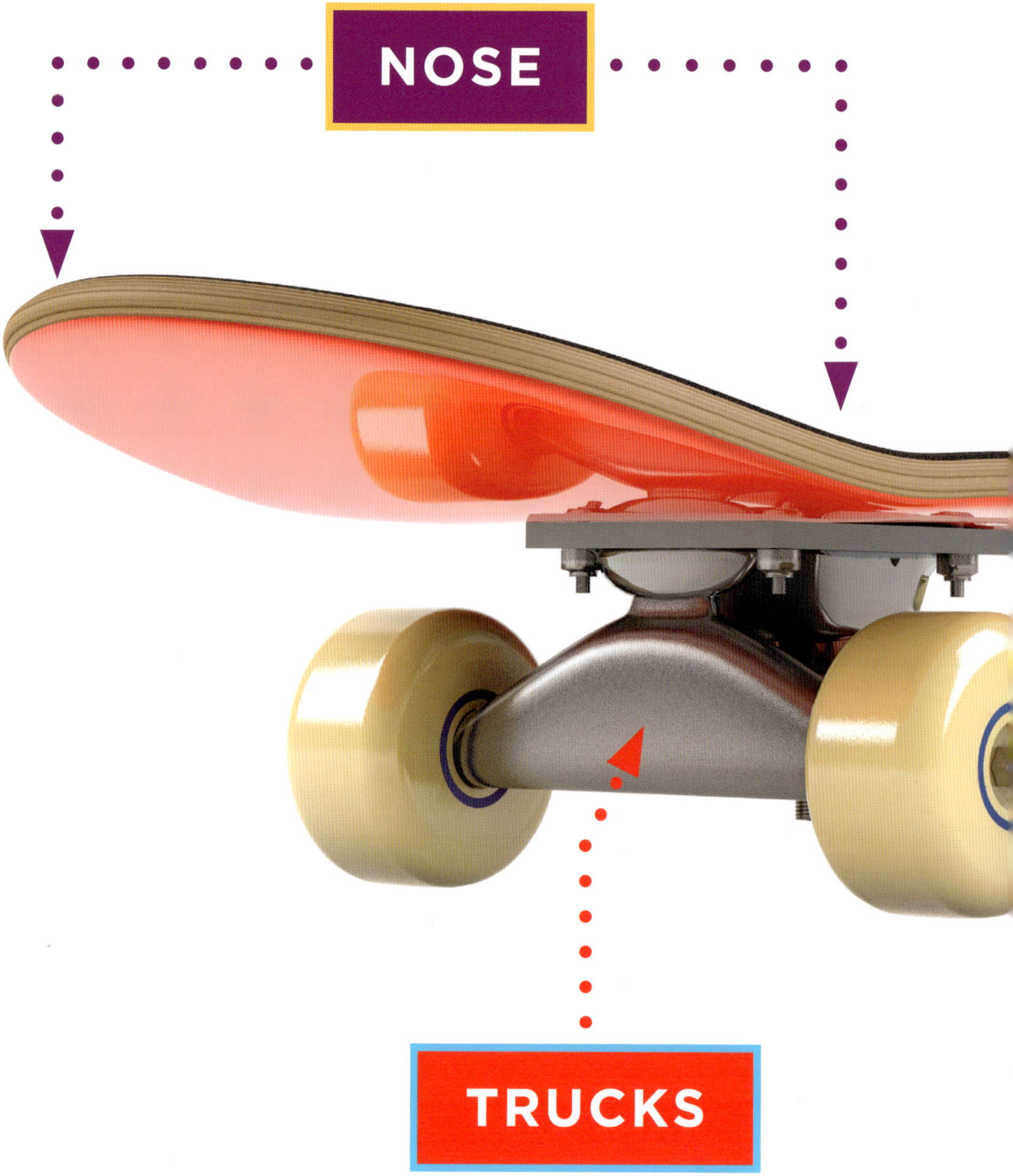

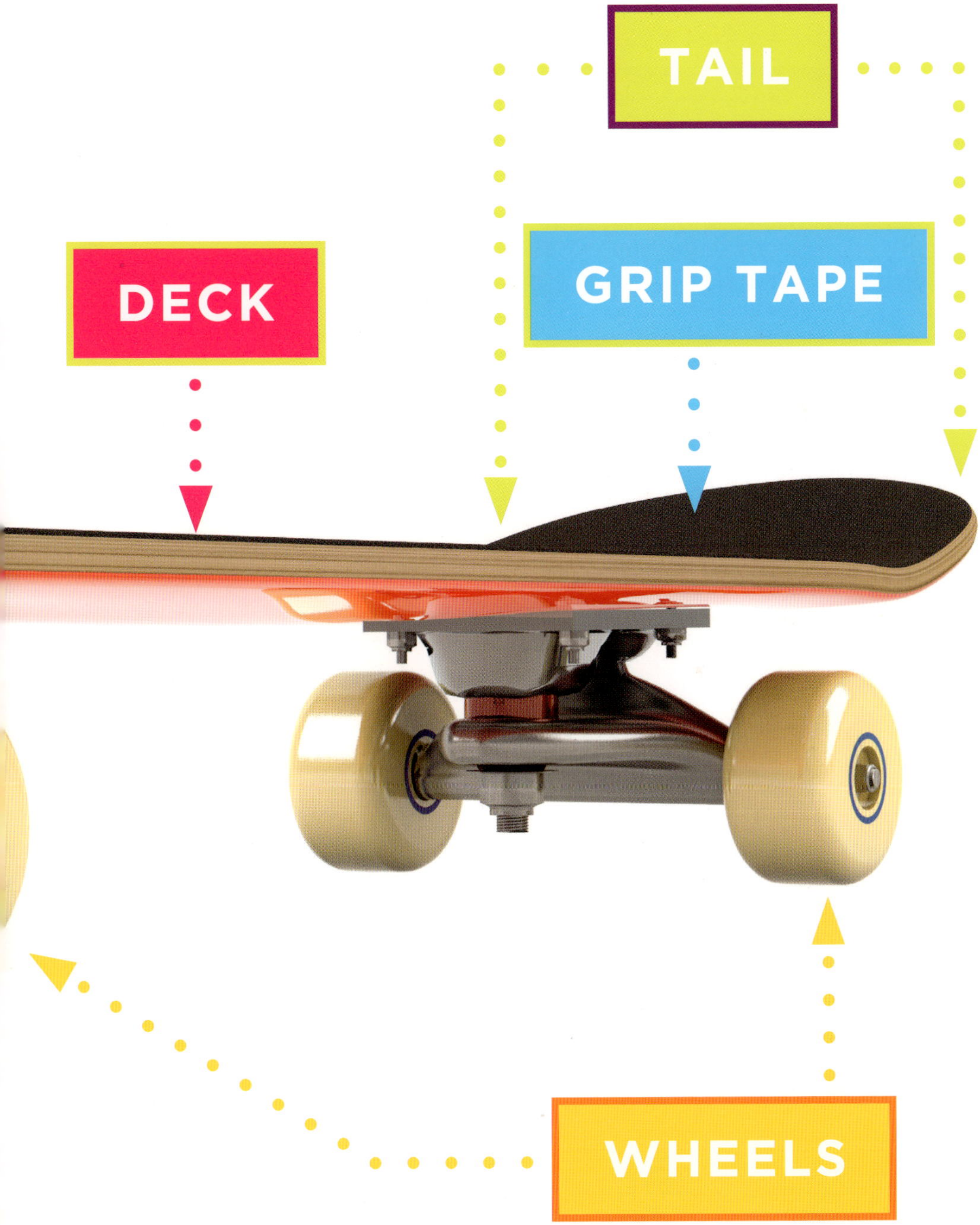
TAIL
DECK
GRIP TAPE
WHEELS

Why Skateboard?

Skateboarders often show off tricks. Beginners aim to ollie. This basic trick pops the board into the air. It leads to more advanced tricks. Then skateboarders try kickflips or grinds on **obstacles**.

Advanced skateboarders may test themselves on the half-pipe. This is where the most extreme tricks happen. Skateboarders speed up the ramp. They twist and turn as they catch air.

How to Do an Ollie

Where to Skateboard?

Skateboarders use city objects around town. They grind along curbs. They ollie over stairs. But skateparks are the best places. They have many obstacles all in one area. Some parks have a bowl that skaters drop into. They ride along the walls. There may be a separate area for bigger ramps.

Skateboard Slang

goofy
to push off with your left foot

wipe out
to fall during a trick

sketchy
a trick that is not done well

regular
to push off with your right foot

raspberries
also known as road rash; scrapes from falling on pavement

SKATEPARK ELEMENTS

half-pipe
bank
rail

CHAPTER 3

Gearing Up

Along with a board, skateboarders need protective gear. Falls can be painful. A mistake could lead to road rash, sprains, or even broken bones. Skateboarders wear helmets and pads. They also wear flat skate shoes that grip their boards.

Safety Gear

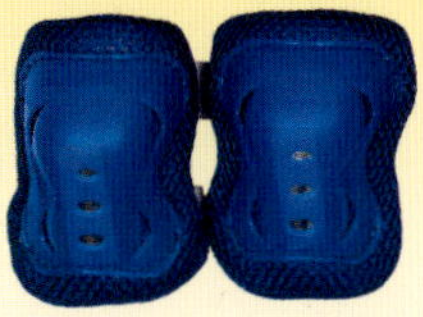

elbow pads

helmet

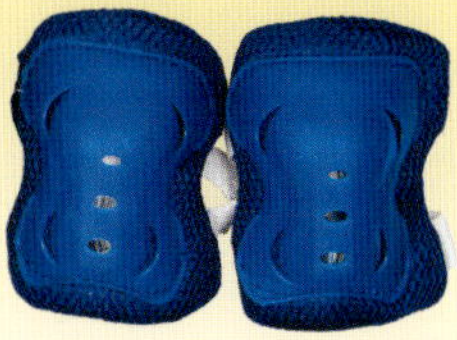

knee pads

skate shoes

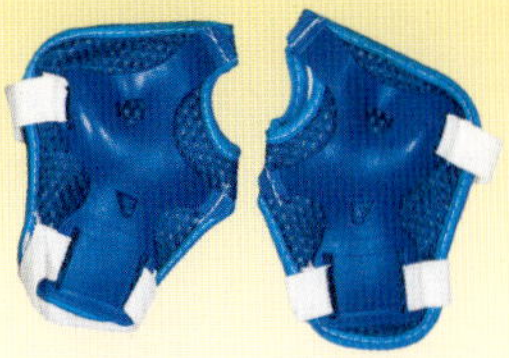

wrist guards

CHAPTER 4

Competitions

The X Games started in 1995. It helped make skateboarding more popular. The event includes vert skateboarding. Skateboarders take several runs on this high half-pipe. They do grabs, spins, and flips. Judges rate the tricks. The highest score wins!

Park Competition

Street Competition

An Olympic Sport

In 2021, skateboarding joined in the Olympics. There are two events for men and women. In the park competition, skateboarders do tricks in a skatepark. They ride bowls and catch air on quarter-pipes. For the street competition, skateboarders do tricks on city obstacles. They fly down rails and jump over stairs.

Skateboard Records

10 years old
age of youngest skateboarder to turn pro, set by **Sky Brown**

1260-degrees
longest turn to date; first completed by **Mitchie Brusco**

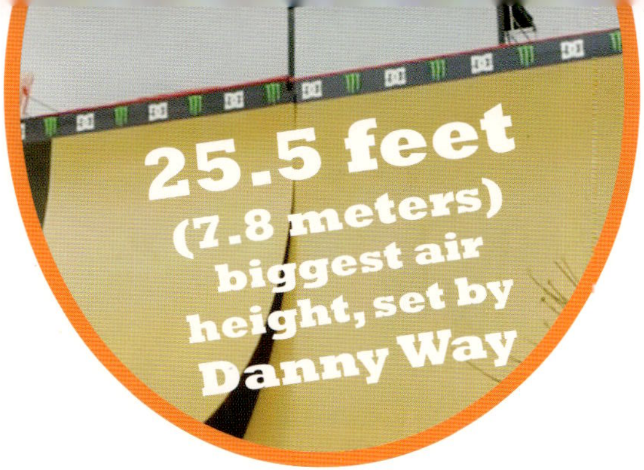

25.5 feet
(7.8 meters)
biggest air height, set by Danny Way

91 miles
(146 kilometers)
per hour
fastest downhill speed set by Pete Connelly

30 Bob Burnquist

Most X Games medals

12 Letícia Bufoni

Downhill Racing

Downhill racing is scary fast. Skateboarders easily top speeds of 50 miles (80 km) per hour on straight parts. They turn their boards sideways to slow down around corners. First one to the bottom wins!

Spills can be rough at these speeds. Skateboarders wear hip pads. They use slide gloves to keep their balance.

MONS ND PROUD.

DAGGER SKATEBOARDS
GAMES

Big Air

Big air events push the limits of what skateboarders can do. Skaters speed down a huge ramp that can be as long as a football field. They launch as high as 50 feet (15 m) into the air. They perform wild tricks with many twists and turns. Then they try to hit a clean landing.

From speed to big air, skateboarding has high thrills and risk. Pros are always pushing to see what extreme trick they can land next.

360—a turn that goes in a full circle

bomb (BOM)—to ride down a big hill at fast speeds

fakie (FEYK-ee)—to ride backwards

half-pipe (HAF-pahyp)—a U-shaped high-sided ramp or runway used to provide a takeoff for a jump

kickturn (KIK-turn)—to balance a skateboard on its back wheels and turn the front of the board in a different direction

obstacle (OB-stuh-kuhl)—an object to go around or over

BOOKS

Conaghan, Bernard. *Skateboarding.* New York: Crabtree Publishing, 2023.

Lyon, Drew. *Downhill Skateboarding and Other Extreme Skateboarding.* North Mankato, Minn.: Capstone Press, 2022.

Wolny, Philip. *Extreme Skateboarding.* New York: Rosen Publishing, 2020.

WEBSITES

38+ Easy Beginner Skateboard Tricks That Look Impressive
www.skateboardershq.com/easy-beginner-skateboard-tricks-which-look-impressive/

Skateboarding
kids.britannica.com/kids/article/skateboarding/437407

Skateboarding
kids.kiddle.co/Skateboarding

INDEX